MISTER UNFUNNY

AT CHRISTMAS TIME

Roger Mee-Senseless

DISCLAIMER:

This is not a Mr Men book.
It is unsuitable for
young children.

If, however, you have the sense
of humour of a 7 year old and
are simply trapped in an
adult's body then it will
be entirely suitable.

Critical acclaim for Mister Unfunny-

"THE FUNNIEST THING I'VE SEEN SINCE LAST TUESDAY, WHEN I SAW SOMEONE WALK INTO A LAMP POST."
BARRY IRELAND, BARRY ISLAND

"I LAUGHED SO MUCH THAT A LITTLE BIT OF DRIBBLE CAME OUT OF MY NOSE, I SHOULD PROBABLY GO TO THE DOCTORS ABOUT THAT ACTUALLY."
IVOR SOREBOTTOM, WETWANG

"WOULD MAKE A GREAT PRESENT FOR SOMEONE YOU DON'T LIKE VERY MUCH."
POLLY VINYL-CHLORIDE, CRUDWELL

Mr Unfunny was a profoundly unfunny man.

Only two people in MisterandMissusland thought that Mr Unfunny was actually funny and those two people were Mister Bonehead (who had an IQ of 3.5, the same as a piece of wet cardboard) and Mr Unfunny himself.

In his own mind he was the most hilarious person to walk the Earth and he would often send himself into fits of laughter with one of his 'top tier' jokes like 'What do you get if you cross Santa and a duck?'

merry christmas ya filthy animal
a christmas quacker

So, you get an idea of his level.
Christmas was Mr Unfunny's favourite time of year. He just loved all of the potential material for jokes and everyone seemed to be in a more jovial mood.

Well, everyone apart from Mr Unfunny's long suffering family who had to put up with his 'unique sense of humour'. Mr Unfunny's son, Timmy, had grown tired of his dad's jokes. When he was 4 he found them quite funny but now at the age of 5 he found them to be too immature.

He'd told his dad as much and his wife, Mrs Unfunny had pleaded with him to reign it in this year.

When she'd told him this he fell into fits of laughter screaming,

"HAHAHAHAHAHA, reign it in, like RUDOLPH! HAAAAAAAAAA. I'm going to use that one! Thanks!"

One day the Unfunny household awoke to a fresh blanket of snow. Timmy was especially excited and hurriedly got his wellies and gloves on and rushed outside.

5 minutes later his mum called him back in to put some pants and trousers on.

When he was actually dressed he sent his friend, Tommy, a text message so that he could come and help build a snowman.

After about half an hour they were making good progress and had nearly finished. At this point Mr Unfunny came outside to 'inspect their handiwork'.

"Not bad," he said. "You've got the proportions about right I reckon." All the while that he was speaking Timmy was bracing himself for the inevitable embarrassment of ANOTHER terrible joke. But to his amazement none came. Mr Unfunny went back indoors without so much as a knock, knock joke!

Two minutes passed and Timmy heard a voice calling from the upstairs bedroom window -

"OF COURSE, IF YOU GAVE YOUR SNOWMAN A SIX-PACK THEN HE WOULD BE THE ABDOMINAL SNOWMAN!"

Mr Unfunny guffawed.

It wasn't just Mr Unfunny's family that fell victim to his jokes. Nobody was safe. Heading out to buy some Christmas presents he selected a soft penguin toy for one of his nephews.

Not being able to resist the opportunity he asked the girl on the till, "What do you call a penguin in the Sahara Desert?"
The girl stared blankly.
"Lost!"
She continued to stare blankly as she gave Mr Unfunny his change.
'Well that was a waste of £20,' thought Mr Unfunny to himself, who had specifically bought the penguin so that he could tell the joke.

SAHARA DESERT
SOUTH POLE
8000 miles

"Right, that's it, I'm off somewhere that my sense of humour is appreciated," said Mr Unfunny one day.

"So you're going around to Mr Bonehead's then?" quipped Mrs Unfunny.

"No, actually. I do have other friends you know! I'll be back late," said Mr Unfunny as he left the house, slamming the door as he left like a petulant child.

He had to sheepishly ring the doorbell 10 seconds later because he'd forgotten his coat. And then again for his keys.

25 minutes later Mr Unfunny arrived at Mr Bonehead's house. Mr Unfunny decided to conduct a test - lots of people had said that Mr Bonehead would laugh at ANYTHING, apparently he would even laugh when reading the ingredients on a packet of crisps but Mr Unfunny prayed that this was untrue.

"Knock, knock," said Mr Unfunny.
"Ohhh, I like these," said Mr Bonehead, "Who's there?"
"Boris," replied Mr Unfunny.
"Boris who?"
"Boris Johnson."

Silence.

"So it isn't true, he doesn't laugh at everything!" thought Mr Unfunny to himself.

But then:

"HAHAHAHAHAHAHAHAHAHAHAHAHAHAHAHAHAHA HAHAHAHAHAHAH!" screamed Mr Bonehead.

Mr Unfunny was pretty confused. "Why are you laughing? It's not even a joke?!"

Mr Bonehead was just drying his eyes and once he was able to speak again said, "Yeh, but imagine if Boris Johnson knocked on your door!"

HA HA HA
HA HA
HA HA,
I DON'T
GET IT.

"It would be hilarious!" he continued.

"Hmmmm," said Mr Unfunny coming to the slow realisation that his best friend was as everyone else said - a buck toothed simpleton.

Mr Unfunny headed back home and on the way called in at his next door neighbour's house. Mr Dump had just moved in and Mr Unfunny was keen to make a good impression. He took an age to answer the door because he was on the toilet. Mr Dump was always on the toilet.

"Hi Mr Dump, I'm just letting you know out of courtesy that we will be having a Christmas party and that the music might be a bit loud.

"Okay, that's fine," said Mr Dump who was about to close the door.
"Yeh, this will be the 5th year in a row that the in-laws have come over for Christmas. This year we might even let them in!" said Mr Unfunny.

"Oh," said Mr Dump.

"Anyhew, have you heard that Tesco are giving away dead batteries this Christmas? - They're free of charge!"

"Okay, thanks for letting me know," said Mr Dump.

'Has this WHOLE TOWN had a sense of humour bypass?' thought Mr Unfunny.

The following day was the night of little Timmy's school carol service, in which Timmy was starring as an angel. Mrs Unfunny had been looking forwards to it for ages and had made Mr Unfunny promise that he would be on his best behaviour.

When they arrived they took a seat near the front. Soon after a teacher came onto the stage and spoke into the microphone: "Good evening ladies and gentlemen, welcome to our production. We will be with you shortly, we are just attending to a little technical difficulty backstage. Talk amongst yourselves, or perhaps someone knows some good jokes that you could come to the front to tell?" she said jokingly.

"SIT DOWN!" said Mrs Unfunny placing her hand firmly on Mr Unfunny's arm.
"But this could be my big moment. I think it's fate!" said Mr Unfunny.

"It's not fate. One of the children has gone to the toilet in their pants, like the teacher just said.

"But pleeeeeeaaaassseee?" he pleaded.
"If you get on that stage then I'm taking the kids and leaving you," she said.

"So that's a firm no is it?" said Mr Unfunny.

"YES! IT'S A FIRM NO."

Christmas Day soon arrived and after
all of the usual present opening stuff
the family set about preparing dinner.

When it was all served they sat around
the table and pulled some crackers.
Timmy pulled his and unfolded the joke
written inside. "What's orange and
sounds like a parrot?" he asked.
"A carrot!" screamed Mr Unfunny.
"Unbelievable, they've stolen MY joke."

The family all looked at each other and
rolled their eyes.

"Timmy, where are those crackers from?
I'm going to sue them for damages."

"It just says 'Made in China'."
"Well, I'll sue them then."
"You can't sue China for that," said Mrs Unfunny.
"You just watch me. When they get a letter from the small claims court they'll crap themselves."
"Do you not think that joke has been around for years?" probed Mrs Unfunny.
"No, I do not. I invented it and what's more I can prove it. Look it's right here in my own joke book. That's indisputable evidence right there. I'm already planning what I'm going to spend the money on."
"Comedy lessons?" suggested Timmy.
"Pardon?" said Mr Unfunny.
"Nothing," replied Timmy.

My Mega
JOKE
Book by
Mr Unfunny
aged 38 ½
KEEP OUT

After dinner the most important part of the day (for Mr Unfunny at least) had arrived - the annual family talent show. Unsurprisingly he took it pretty seriously and announced each 'act' as if he was the MC in the middle of a boxing ring.

His credibility was undermined somewhat as he was using his 3 year old daughter's battery powered Barbie microphone. The line up for the competition this year was pretty strong. Mrs Unfunny's mum was first up, being the eldest.

"Maureen, what's your act?" Mr Unfunny whispered to her while holding his hand over the microphone to dampen it.

(He did this so that everyone else sat in the room, 2 metres away, wouldn't be able to hear. It didn't work.)

Maureen whispered back.

"PLEASE WELCOME TO THE BIG ANNUAL CHRISTMAS TALENT SHOW EXTRAVAGANZA MAUREEN, WHO IS GOING TO SEE HOW FAST SHE CAN FALL ASLEEP IN FRONT OF WALLACE AND GROMIT!"

Timmy followed this with a pretty solid routine with his nose flute and Mrs Unfunny 'entertained' the audience by crocheting an entire cardigan in *only* 2 and a half hours.

Then it was Tilly's turn. She'd put together a show starring her dolls where she put on a variety of voices for the different characters.

Mrs Unfunny and her mum welled up watching it. Well, Maureen was asleep but if she'd been awake she would surely have welled up.

Mr Unfunny, keen to get on with his own act wasn't quite so charitable. "I'm sorry Tilly, I'm finding this plot quite implausible and to be honest it's all quite derivative. Can you wind it up please?"

Then it was the turn of Mr Unfunny himself...

"AND NOW, THE MAIN EVENT. THE ACT THAT YOU'VE ALL BEEN WAITING FOR. PLEASE WELCOME TO THE STAGE – THE MAN, THE MYTH, THE LEGEND, THE WALKING JOKE MACHINE .IT'S MEEEEEEEE!!!!"

Mr Unfunny stepped into the middle of the room through the haze of a smoke machine that he had bought especially for his act. He felt like it was 1997 and he was on 'Stars in Their Eyes' with Matthew Kelly.

For the next half an hour he proceeded to recite his entire back catalogue of 'top tier jokes', which included...

WHY HAS SANTA BEEN BANNED FROM SOOTY CHIMNEYS?

BECAUSE OF CARBON FOOTPRINTS.

WHAT DO YOU GET IF YOU EAT CHRISTMAS DECORATIONS?

TINSELITIS.

AT CHRISTMAS, MOTHER SAYS TO LITTLE JOHNNY, "GO ON AND LIGHT UP THE CHRISTMAS TREE JOHNNY."

JOHNNY RUNS OFF HAPPILY AND COMES BACK AFTER A WHILE, ASKING, "SHOULD I LIGHT UP THE CANDLES, TOO?"

and

WHAT DID THE FARMER GET FOR CHRISTMAS?

A COWCULATOR

A COWCULATOR

$5 + 10 =$ ~~510~~ → 25

9^2

$7 \overline{)42}$ 6

$\pi = 3.14$

$9 \times 5 = 45$

$70 - 52$

Mr Unfunny delivered the jokes with all of the gusto that he could manage. When he'd finished he marched out of the living room like he was leaving the stage of the London Palladium. Only to re-enter 3 seconds later so that the family could all submit their scores to decide the big winner.

Unbelievably, he hadn't won. He demanded a recount, sure that a mistake had been made, so Mrs Unfunny counted out the voting slips in front of him. "One, two, three. Three votes for Maureen (who had fallen asleep in a very impressive 42 seconds).

"Maybe you should find some new material, you have told each one of these jokes at least 5,000 times after all," offered Mrs Unfunny.

"You know, you might be right. Maybe I'm just actually not that funny," said Mr Unfunny. Mrs Unfunny smiled weakly but with a glint of hopefulness in her eyes. Maybe Mr Unfunny was about to have a life changing revealtion.

"Or...." said Mr Unfunny, "Maybe people just aren't quite ready for my humour. I'm going to start practising for next year right now! Happy Christmas!"

WIN WIN WIN!

If you enjoyed this book then please consider leaving a review on Amazon. Doing so will automatically enter you into a competition to win a year's supply of chicken beaks.

(where's me beak gone?)

Printed in Great Britain
by Amazon